Not for All the
HAMANTASCHEN
in Town

With love to Jason, Adam, Mara, Leah, and Ken
—L.A.M.

For my lovable piglets, for my husband
Rostislav and for my daughter Eve
—I.C.

KAR-BEN PUBLISHING
An imprint of Lerner Publishing Group, Inc.
241 First Avenue North
Minneapolis, MN 55401 USA
1-800-4-KARBEN

Website address: www.karben.com

Main body text set in Chaloops. Typeface provided by Chank.

Library of Congress Cataloging-in-Publication Data

Milhander, Laura Aron, author.
Not for all the hamantaschen in town / by Laura Aron Milhander ; illustrated by Inna Chernyak.
pages cm
Summary: "Rishon, Sheni, and Shlishi make crowns for the Purim parade, but Rishon and Sheni hurry through theirs so they can go play. When the big, bad wolf shows up at the Purim carnival looking for hamantaschen, things go awry as he tries to steal a costume"— Provided by publisher.
ISBN 978-1-4677-5928-1 (lb : alk. paper)
ISBN 978-1-4677-5930-4 (pb : alk. paper)
ISBN 978-1-4677-9613-2 (eb pdf)
[1. Pigs—Fiction. 2. Wolves—Fiction. 3. Purim—Fiction. 4. Conduct of life—Fiction.] I. Chernyak, Inna, illustrator. II. Title.
PZ7.1.M557No 2016
[E]—dc23 2015016340

Manufactured in China
2-53379-17988-5/23/2022

0223/B0769/A6

Not for All the HAMANTASCHEN in Town

Laura Aron Milhander

Illustrated by

Inna Chernyak

KAR-BEN PUBLISHING

Once upon a time there were three little pigs who lived together in a sturdy brick house. The pigs worked hard during the week, and on the weekends they relaxed by wallowing in the cool, smooth mud.

One morning, the pigs were getting ready for Purim.

"The Purim carnival is tomorrow!" exclaimed the first pig, whose name was Rishon. "It will be so much fun!"

"We'll need costumes," said the second pig, Sheni.

"Let's make crowns!" suggested Shlishi, the third pig. "We can all be King Ahasuerus in the Purim parade!"

The three little pigs collected their craft supplies to make crowns for the carnival.

Rishon made his crown out of bright purple paper. It only took him a few minutes, and he spent the rest of the afternoon playing in the mud.

Sheni made his crown with poster board, gold foil, and glue. This took a little longer, but there was still plenty of time for a dip in the mud with Rishon.

Shlishi made his crown from poster board, too, but he had a plan . . .

He decided to make his crown even stronger with papier mache.

First, he cut out his crown from the poster board.

Then he mixed flour and water to form a paste.

Next he dipped strips of newspaper into the paste . . .

. . . and stuck them onto
the poster board crown.

While he waited for the papier mache
to dry, Shlishi cleaned up the mess.

Then he decorated the crown. It took
him all afternoon to finish. He didn't
take even a minute to play in the mud
before it was time to go to bed.

The next morning, Rishon, Sheni, and Shlishi put on their crowns and set out for the Purim carnival.

Meanwhile, a big, bad wolf was prowling the forest outside of town.

“Mmmm, I smell hamantaschen. Delicious! I’ll go into town and buy some.”

When the little pigs reached the carnival, they squealed in delight. The street was packed with game booths, prize tables, and food stands. Music, cheering, and laughter echoed all around. Everybody, young and old, was dressed in every imaginable costume.

"Let's split up and explore!" said Rishon. "We can meet by the hamantaschen stand in a little while." So the little pigs all ran off in different directions.

When the wolf arrived in town, everyone who saw him gasped and ran away in fear. The wolf was used to this, but he began to worry. Big, bad wolves would not be welcome at the Purim carnival. What if no one would sell him a hamantaschen?

The wolf noticed the bright and lively costumes everybody was wearing. "If I have a costume, no one will recognize me," he said to himself. "Then no one will be afraid of me, and I'll be able to buy a hamantaschen!"

He had to find a costume quickly. It was too late to make a costume, but perhaps he could steal one!

He came upon Rishon, who was helping to collect baskets of *mishloach manot* for *tzedakah*.

The wolf leaped in front of Rishon and growled, “Little pig, little pig, give me your crown!”

“Not for all the hamantaschen in town!” exclaimed Rishon.

“Then I’ll huff and I’ll puff, and I’ll blow your crown off!”

And that's just what he did. The crown, made only of paper, flew off Rishon's head.

But before the wolf could grab it, the crown was caught by the passing breeze and disappeared down the street. The wolf gave a small, sad howl and rushed off in search of another costume.

The wolf spotted Sheni, who was decorating a Megillah cover at the craft table. The wolf bounded up to Sheni and snarled, "Little pig, little pig, give me your crown!"

"Not for all the hamantaschen in town!" cried Sheni.

"Then I'll huff and I'll puff, and I'll blow your crown off!"

And that's just what the wolf did. Cardboard is stronger than paper, but after the second puff, the crown flew off Sheni's head. Before the wolf could grab it, some children ran past and trampled it beneath their feet. The wolf sighed and ran off again.

The wolf noticed Shlishi among a crowd of children practicing making noise with their groggers. The wolf jumped in front of Shlishi and howled, "Little pig, little pig, give me your crown!"

"Not for all the hamantaschen in town!" shouted Shlishi.

"Then I'll huff and I'll puff, and I'll blow your crown off!"

And . . . he tried. Again and again the wolf blew, but the sturdy crown stayed on Shlishi's head. Finally the wolf reached out to grab the crown with his paws . . .

Just then, a child stepped forward. "If you want a costume, you can use my hat." He offered the wolf a black, three-cornered Haman hat.

The wolf eagerly placed it on his head between his furry ears. The other children, seeing the wolf dressed as Haman, booed and shook their groggers.

"Oh no!" cried the wolf. "Nobody likes Haman, and nobody likes me! I'll never get a hamantaschen!"

The embarrassed wolf turned to run away, but Shlishi stopped him. "If you want a hamantaschen, you don't need a costume. And you don't need to be a bully either. You just need to ask nicely."

"But I'm a big, bad wolf!" the wolf protested.

"You may be big," said Shlishi, "but you don't have to be bad. Here—I'll lend you my crown." Shlishi took off his crown and handed it to the wolf.

“Thank you,” stammered the wolf. He exchanged his Haman hat for Shlishi’s crown, and the children cheered.

“I’m sorry about all the huffing and puffing,” the wolf mumbled.

“We forgive you,” said a lamb dressed as Queen Esther. “Come on! The hamantaschen stand is this way.”

So the wolf got his hamantaschen. And when it was time for the Purim parade, he politely thanked Shlishi again and returned his crown.

That evening, the three little pigs made their way home—tired, happy, and full of hamantaschen. But only Shlishi still had his wonderful crown.

(NOT FOR ALL THE) HAMANTASCHEN RECIPE

INGREDIENTS:

¾ cup (170 g) butter
¾ cup (170 g) sour cream
1–1½ cup (300 g) sugar
2 eggs
4 cups (500 g) flour
1 tsp. baking powder
1 tsp. baking soda
¼ tsp. salt
Fillings of your choice—
poppyseed, apricot jam,
chocolate chips or other

Preheat oven to 350° F (177° C). Cream butter. Add sugar gradually and beat until fluffy. Add eggs one at a time. Add sour cream and stir. Sift dry ingredients together. Stir into dough. Chill one hour. Roll out dough until ⅛ inch (0.3 cm) thick. Cut into circles with cookie cutter or bottom of drinking glass. Fill with choice of filling. Shape into triangles. Bake 10-15 minutes until lightly browned.

Makes 3-4 dozen depending on size.

Eat and enjoy. Happy Purim!

ABOUT PURIM

Purim, a holiday that comes in early spring, celebrates how brave Queen Esther saved the Jewish people of Persia from wicked Haman's evil plot to destroy them. The story is told in the biblical Book of Esther. Families celebrate by wearing costumes, eating three-cornered cookies called hamantaschen, listening to the reading of the Megillah (a scroll containing the story) and making noise with groggers, blotting out the name of the villain Haman.

GLOSSARY

grogger: a noisemaker, used at Purim to drown out the sound of Haman's name whenever it is mentioned during the reading of the Megillah

hamantaschen: a triangle-shaped pastry traditionally filled with poppy seeds or jam

mishloach manot: a basket of treats given to friends and neighbors on Purim

Megillah: scroll containing the story of Purim

rishon: first

sheni: second

shlishi: third

tzedakah: charity, which is seen as an obligation—not just a good deed—for Jewish people